THE SPIDERWICK CHRONICLES

GREAT ESCAPE
SPECIAL EDITION OF
THE SEEING STONE

VOLUME THREE

with EXCLUS~~~~

Tony DiTerl~~~~

Simon and Schuster Books for Young Readers

New York London Toronto Sydney

SIMON & SCHUSTER BOOKS FOR YOUNG READERS
An imprint of Simon & Schuster Children's Publishing Division
1230 Avenue of the Americas, New York, New York 10020

Table of Contents

THE
JUNKYARD

THE
CAMP

THE
BRIDGE

ROUNTREE STREET

THE
SPIDERWICK
ESTATE

DULAC DRIVE

THE
GROVE

TO TOWN

THE OLD QUARRY

J. WATERHOUSE MIDDLE SCHOOL

RIGGENBACH WAY

ROBINSON CREEK

N

Map of the
SPIDERWICK
ESTATE
and Surrounding Areas

Welcome to our daring tale,
but there's a little twist:
This book is not the very start.
That's right. There's stuff you missed!

THE GRACE KIDS

So let us take you back in time,
back to our starting place,
where you can meet our heroes three—
Mallory, Simon, and Jared Grace.

They'd left the city far behind
and moved out to the sticks,
to a musty, dusty old estate
with the name of SPIDERWICK.

A. SPIDERWICK

And no sooner had they settled in
than mysteries arose.
A secret room! A long-lost book!
A houseguest filled with woes!

And, oh, the woe this creature caused!
And, oh, the grief and shame,
for every prank this rascal pulled,
poor Jared got the blame.

THE BOGGART

But that lost book was filled with clues.
When found, it set things right.
And in that secret room a brownie
stepped into the light.

He cautioned our young heroes three
of troubles deep and drastic
if they kept the book, Spiderwick's guide
to worlds close and fantastic.

THIMBLETACK

But young Jared heeded not,
saw nothing to be feared,
until before his very eyes
his brother disappeared.

He asked the brownie Thimbletack
for aid finding a stone
that saw into the hidden world
in which his twin had gone.

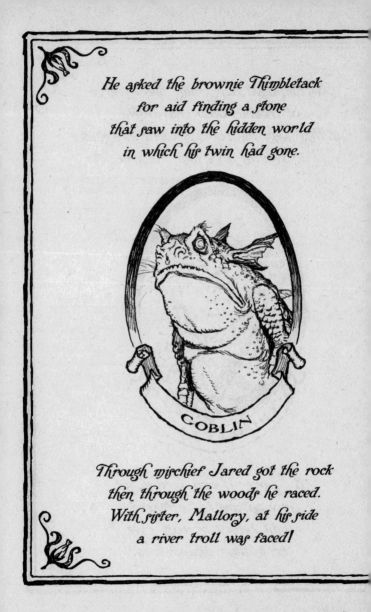

GOBLIN

Through mischief Jared got the rock
then through the woods he raced.
With sister, Mallory, at his side
a river troll was faced!

Anon, a goblin camp was found
with Simon (and a friend),
which means the best is yet to come,
escape and home again.

TROLL

So while our tale is almost done,
the danger's not diminished.
Oh, yes! There's still a task or two
before this tale is finished!

The flames blazed green.

Chapter One

IN WHICH Jared Is Forced to Make a Difficult Choice

*L*et me OUT!" Hogsqueal yelled. Jared snapped into motion and cut through the last knot.

Hogsqueal danced onto the branch, heedless of the goblins barking beneath him. They had begun to surround the tree.

Jared looked around for some kind of weapon, but all he had was his little knife. Simon was breaking off more branches and Hogsqueal was running away, jumping from tree to tree like a monkey. He and his brother were abandoned and trapped. If they tried to climb down, the goblins would be upon them.

And somewhere down there, in the gloom, Mallory was alone and blind. Her only protection was the red of the sweatshirt she wore.

"What about the animals in the cages?" Simon asked.

"No time!"

"Hey, mucky-pups!" Jared heard Hogsqueal shout. He looked in the direction of the voice, but Hogsqueal wasn't talking to them at all. He was dancing around the campfire and sticking a large strip of burnt rat meat in his mouth.

"Ninnyhammers!" he yelled at the other goblins. "Pestleheads! Goobernuts! Jibbernolls! Fiddlewizzits!" He leaned back and spat into the fire, making the flames blaze green.

The goblins turned from the tree and headed right for Hogsqueal.

"Move!" Jared said. "Now!"

Simon climbed down the tree as fast as he could, jumping once he was close enough. He fell to the ground with a soft thud. Jared landed beside him.

Mallory hugged them both, but she didn't let go of her stick.

"I heard the goblins get close, but I couldn't see a thing," she said.

"Put this on." Jared held out the eyepiece to her.

"You need it," she protested.

"Now!" Jared said.

Surprisingly Mallory buckled it on without another word. After it was on, she reached into her sweatshirt and gave Simon back the shoe he had lost between the river and the goblin camp.

They started moving into the woods, but Jared couldn't help looking back. Hogsqueal was surrounded.

They couldn't leave him like that.

"Hey!" he called. "Over here!"

The goblins turned and, seeing the three children, started moving toward them.

Jared, Mallory, and Simon started to run.

"Are you crazy?" Mallory yelled.

"He was helping us," Jared yelled back. He couldn't be sure she'd heard him since he was panting at the same time he was speaking.

"Where are we going?" Simon shouted.

"The stream," said Jared. He was thinking fast, faster than he'd ever thought in his life. The troll was their only chance. He was sure that it could stop ten goblins with no problem. What he wasn't sure of was how they could avoid it themselves.

"We can't go this way," Mallory said. Jared ignored her.

If only they could jump the stream, maybe

that would be enough. The goblins wouldn't know there was a monster to avoid.

The goblins were still far enough behind. They wouldn't see what was coming.

Almost there. Jared could see the stream ahead, but they weren't to the ruined bridge yet.

Then Jared saw something that stopped him cold. The troll was out of the water. It stood at the edge of the bank, eyes and teeth gleaming in the moonlight. Even hunched over, Jared guessed that it was more than ten feet tall.

"Luckyyyy meee," it said, reaching out a long arm in their direction.

"Wait," said Jared.

The creature moved toward them, a slow smile showing broken teeth. It definitely was not waiting.

"Hear that?" Jared asked. "That's goblins.

17

It stood at the edge of the bank.

Ten fat goblins. That's a lot more than three skinny kids."

The monster hesitated. The Guide had said that trolls weren't very smart. Jared hoped that was true.

"All you have to do is get back in the stream and we'll lead them right to you. I promise."

The yellow eyes of the creature glinted greedily. "Yesss," it said.

"Hurry!" Jared said. "They're almost here!"

It slid toward the water and dropped under with barely a ripple.

"What was that?" Simon asked.

Jared was shaking, but he could not let that stop him. "Go in the stream there, where it's shallow. We have to get them to chase us through the water."

"Are you nuts?" Mallory demanded.

"Please," Jared begged. "Trust me."

"We have to do something!" said Simon.

"Okay, let's go." Mallory followed her brothers toward the muddy bank, shaking her head.

The goblins burst through the trees. Jared, Mallory, and Simon waded through the shallow water, zigzagging around the pit. The fastest way to go after them would be to cut through the middle of the stream.

Jared heard the goblins splashing behind them, barking madly. Then the barks turned to squeals. Jared looked back to see a few goblins paddling for the shore. The troll grabbed them

all, shaking and biting and dragging them down to his watery lair.

Jared tried not to look any more. His stomach did an odd, nauseous flip-flop.

Simon looked pale and a little queasy.

"Let's go home," Mallory said.

Jared nodded.

"We can't," said Simon. "What about all those animals?"

The full moon overhead

Chapter Two

IN WHICH Simon Outdoes Himself and Finds an Extraordinary New Pet

"Y ou have to be kidding," Mallory said when Simon explained what he wanted to do.

"They're going to die if we don't," Simon insisted. "The griffin is bleeding."

"The griffin, too?" Jared asked. He understood about the cats, but a griffin?

"How are we going to help that thing?" Mallory demanded. "We're not faerie veterinarians!"

"We have to try," said Simon just as firmly.

Jared owed it to Simon to agree. After all, he had put Simon through a lot. "We could get the old tarp from the carriage house."

"Yeah," Simon chimed in. "Then we could drag the griffin back to the house. There's plenty of room."

Mallory rolled her eyes.

"If it lets us," Jared said. "Did you see what it did to that goblin?"

"Come on, guys," Simon pleaded. "I'm not strong enough to pull it alone."

"All right," she said. "But I'm not standing close to the head."

Jared, Simon, and Mallory trooped back to the carriage house. The full moon overhead gave them enough light to navigate the woods, but they were still careful, crossing the stream where it was barely a trickle. At the edge of the lawn, Jared could see that the windows of the

24

main house were lit and that his mother's car was parked in the gravel driveway. Was she making dinner? Had she called the police? Jared wanted to go inside and tell his mom that they were all okay, but he didn't dare.

"Jared, come on." Simon had opened the door to the carriage house, and Mallory was pulling the tarp from the old car.

"Hey, look at this." Simon picked up a flashlight from one of the shelves and flicked it on. Luckily, no beam of light spread across the lawn.

"Batteries are probably dead," Jared said.

"Stop playing around," Mallory told them. "We're trying *not* to get caught."

They dragged the tarp back through the woods. The walk went more slowly and with a good deal of arguing about the shortest way. Jared couldn't keep from jumping at distant

25

night noises. Even the croaking of frogs sounded ominous. He couldn't help wondering what else there was, hidden in the dark. Maybe something worse than goblins or trolls. He shook his head

26

and reminded himself that no one could possibly be that unlucky in one day.

When they finally found the goblin camp again, Jared was surprised to see Hogsqueal sitting by the fire. He was licking bones and burped contentedly when they approached.

"I guess you're okay," Jared said.

"Is that any way to talk to someone who saved your prawnheaded hide?"

Jared started to protest—they'd almost gotten killed over the stupid goblin—but Mallory grabbed his arm.

"Help Simon with the animals," she said. "I'll watch the goblin."

"I'm not a goblin," Hogsqueal said. "I'm a *hob*goblin."

"Whatever," said Mallory, sitting on a rock.

Simon and Jared climbed the trees, letting out all the animals in the cages. Most ran down the nearest branch or sprang for the ground, as afraid of the boys as they were of the goblins. One little kitten crouched in the back of a cage, mewling pitifully. Jared didn't know what to do with it, so he put it in his backpack and kept moving. There was no sign of Tibbs.

When Simon saw the kitten, he insisted that they keep it. Jared wished that he meant instead of the griffin.

Jared thought that Hogsqueal's eyes softened when he saw

GRIFFIN

28

the cat, but that might have been from hunger.

When the cages were empty, the three siblings and the hobgoblin approached the griffin. It watched them warily, extending its claws.

Mallory dropped her end of the tarp. "You know, hurt animals sometimes just attack."

"Sometimes they don't, though," said Simon, walking toward the griffin with open hands. "Sometimes they just let you take care of them. I found a rat like that once. It only bit me when it got better."

"Only a bunch of chuckleheads would mess with a wounded griffin." Hogsqueal cracked open another bone and started sucking out the marrow. "You want me to hold that kitten?"

Mallory scowled at him. "You want to follow your friends to the bottom of the stream?"

Jared smiled. It was good to have Mallory on their side.

29

That made him think of something. "Since you're feeling so generous, how about a little goblin spit for my sister?"

"It's *bob*goblin spit," Hogsqueal said loftily.

"Gee, thanks," Mallory said, "but I'll pass."

"No, look—it gives you the Sight. And that even makes sense," Jared said. "I mean, if faerie bathwater works, then this should too."

"I can't even begin to express how disgusting those choices are."

"Well, if that's how she feels about it." Hogsqueal was apparently trying to look offended. Jared didn't think he was succeeding at it too well, because he was licking a bone at the same time.

"Mal, come on. You can't wear a stone strapped to your head all the time."

"Says you," she replied. "Do you even know how long this spit is going to last?"

Jared hadn't really considered that. He looked at Hogsqueal.

"Until someone pokes out your eyes," the faerie said.

"Well, then great," Jared said, trying to get back some control of the conversation.

Mallory sighed. "Fine, fine." She knelt

"I'm not going to hurt you."

down and removed the monocle. Hogsqeal spit with great relish.

Looking up, Jared noticed that Simon had already gone over to the griffin. He was squatting down beside it and whispering.

"Hello, griffin," Simon was saying in his most soothing voice. "I'm not going to hurt you. We're just going to help you get better. Come on, be good."

The griffin let out a whine like a kettle's whistle. Simon stroked its feathers lightly.

"Go ahead and spread out the tarp," Simon whispered.

The griffin raised itself slightly, opening its beak, but Simon's petting seemed to relax it. It put its head back down on the asphalt.

They unrolled the tarp behind it.

Simon knelt down by its head, talking softly with cooing words. The griffin appeared to be listening, ruffling its feathers as though Simon's whispers might tickle.

Mallory crept up to one side of it and gently took hold of its front paws, and Jared took hold of the back.

"One, two, three," they said together softly, then rolled the griffin onto the tarp. It squawked and flailed its legs, but by that time it was on the canvas.

Then they lifted it as much as they could and began the arduous process of dragging the griffin to the carriage house. It was lighter than Jared expected. Simon suggested that it might have hollow bones like a bird.

"So long, chidderblains," Hogsqueal called after them.

"See you around," Jared called back. He almost wished the hobgoblin was coming with them.

Mallory rolled her eyes.

The griffin did not enjoy its trip. They couldn't lift it up too far, so it got dragged over bumps and bushes a lot. It screeched and squawked and fluttered its good wing. They had to stop and wait for Simon to calm it down and then start dragging again. It seemed to take forever to get the griffin back home.

Once at the carriage house, they had to open the double doors in the back and haul the griffin into one of the horse stalls. It settled in some of the old straw.

Simon knelt down to clean the griffin's wounds as well as he could by moonlight and with only water from the hose. Jared got a bucket and filled it for the griffin to drink. It gulped gratefully.

Even Mallory pitched in, finding a moth-

At the carriage house

eaten blanket to drape over the animal. It almost looked tame, bandaged and sleepy in the carriage house.

Even though Jared thought it was crazy to bring the griffin back there, he had to admit that he was starting to have a little affection for it. More than he had for Hogsqueal, at any rate.

By the time Jared, Simon, and Mallory limped into the house, it was very late. Mallory was still damp from her fall into the stream, and Simon's clothes were scratched nearly to tatters. Jared had grass stains on his pants and scraped elbows from his chase through the woods. But they still had the book and the eyepiece, and Simon was carrying a kitten the color of butterscotch toffee, and all of them were still alive. From where Jared stood, those things counted as huge successes.

Their mother was on the phone when they came in. Her face was blotchy with tears.

"They're here!" She hung up the phone and stared at them for a moment. "Where were you? It is one o'clock in the morning!" She pointed her finger at Mallory. "How could you be so irresponsible?"

Mallory looked over at Jared. Simon, on his other side, looked at him too and clutched the cat to his chest. It suddenly occurred to Jared that they were waiting for him to come up with an excuse.

"Um . . . there was a cat in a tree," Jared started. Simon gave him an encouraging smile. "That cat." Jared indicated the kitten in Simon's arms. "And, you see, Simon climbed up the tree, but the kitten got scared. It climbed up even farther and Simon got stuck. And I ran back and got Mallory."

"And I tried to climb after him," Mallory offered.

"Right," Jared said. "She climbed after him. And then the cat jumped into another tree and Simon climbed after it, but the branch broke and he fell in a stream."

"But his clothes aren't wet," their mother said, scowling.

"Jared means that *I* fell in the stream," Mallory said.

"And my *shoe* fell in the stream," said Simon.

"Yeah," Jared said. "Then Simon caught the cat, but then we had to get them out of the tree without him getting clawed up."

"It took a while," said Simon.

Their mother gave Jared a strange look, but she didn't yell. "You three are grounded for the rest of the month. No playing outside and no more excuses."

Jared opened his mouth to argue, but he

couldn't think of a single thing to say.

As the three of them trooped up the stairs, Jared said, "I'm sorry. I guess that was a pretty pathetic excuse."

Mallory shook her head. "There wasn't much you could say. You couldn't explain what really happened."

"Where did those goblins come from?" Jared asked. "We never even found out what they wanted."

"The Guide," Simon said. "That's what I started to tell you before. They thought I had it."

"But how? How could they know that we found it?"

"You don't think that Thimbletack would have told them, do you?" Mallory asked.

Jared shook his head. "He didn't want us to mess with the book in the first place."

Mallory sighed. "Then how?"

41

"What if someone was watching the house, waiting for us to find the book?"

"Someone or something," Simon added worriedly.

"But why?" Jared asked a little louder than he intended. "What's so important about the book? I mean—could those goblins even read?"

Simon shrugged. "They didn't really say why. They just wanted it."

"Thimbletack was right." Jared opened the door to the room he shared with his twin.

Simon's bed was neatly made, the sheets pulled back and the pillow plumped. But Jared's bed was ruined. The mattress hung from the frame, strewn with feathers and stuffing. The sheets had been ripped to ribbons.

"Thimbletack!" said Jared.

"I told you," said Mallory. "You should never have grabbed that stone."

Find more adventure in
GOBLINS ATTACK
and
TROLL TROUBLE

This episode has found its end,
but please don't close the book—
this chapter's new for those of you
who dare to take a look!

Something better would come along soon.

Lost Chapter
THE GREAT ESCAPE

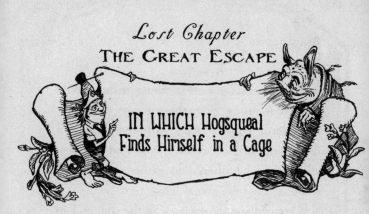

IN WHICH Hogsqueal Finds Himself in a Cage

Hogsqueal whistled a tune and turned to warm his feet by the goblin's fire.

Despite being a hobgoblin, Hogsqueal was sometimes mistook by goblins for one of their kind. That was fine with Hogsqueal. Sure, goblins were nasty and crafty and total numbnoses, but they always knew where to get food. Until something better came along, he was content to doze under the fine new hat he'd discovered and let the goblins do all the work.

And he was sure something better would come along soon. Something always did.

Several goblins were gathered around a dwindling fire of dried leaves and the few sticks they'd bothered to gather. It gave off more smoke than actual flame.

One of them dug around in the soil, picked up a worm, and popped it in its mouth. Sharp glass teeth gobbled it up. Hogsqueal made a face. He was dreaming of fat apples roasted over a fire, not some squirmies. They tasted like dirt.

"When are we going to get some real food?" he said. Sometimes the goblins needed to be reminded of what was important. They weren't exactly big thinkers.

One of the goblins—he called himself Claw, but since there were three others that called themselves Claw, Hogsqueal thought of him as Snotbelly—nosed the air.

"Mmm," Claw-Snotbelly said. "The dump. Fresh meat in the dump!"

"Yes! Yes!" said another goblin, who called herself Flowerbutt. "Meat!"

Hogsqueal pushed himself up and followed with some apprehension. Junkyard food didn't sound all that delicious. As the goblins trooped through the forest with him trailing behind, he considered his options. He could take off and be on his own again, away from these boring wallopheads, but there were trolls and ogres and worse out there just waiting for a juicy hobgoblin to wander too close.

Or he could find someone else to sponge off of—maybe some unsuspecting humans. Some had moved into that old abandoned house on the other side of the stream. They had more food than they knew what to do with. Or maybe he could go to town and target a nice shopkeeper or pet-store owner. Then he'd be set. He smacked his lips, thinking of the possibilities, and then stopped suddenly. They'd reached the gates of the dump.

One of the goblins wiped the drool from its mouth. Even Hogsqueal had to admit that the dump was an impressive sight.

Mountains of old tires and discarded diapers dotted the landscape, each piled with tons and tons of half-eaten food. Delicious food that was just lying around, waiting for someone to eat it. Slightly stale coffee cakes flavored with discarded coffee grounds. Melted puddles of Popsicle sludge. Cheeseburgers still in their wrappers. And climbing around all that garbage were lots of fresh, well-fed rats.

"Maliciously delicious!" he said, all thoughts of sponging off humans evaporating.

He'd been underestimating these goblins. They'd been holding out on him!

The goblins spread out, eating as they went. Flowerbutt bit into a chunk of orange peel. Claw-snotbelly chomped down on a greenish hot dog. The entire junkyard was their all-you-can-eat buffet.

Hogsqueal poked around, searching for choice morsels. Then he saw something else moving around. A quick-moving creature that seemed fluffier than a rat. Maybe a squirrel? He lunged toward it.

What he caught was a kitten. It had a tiny pink nose, orange-striped fur, and huge eyes that reminded him strangely of his own. It looked mouthwatering, but when it meowed plaintively, he tucked it under his hat instead of putting it into his mouth.

"Hey," said Flowerbutt, dropping a brownish

apple core and shuffling over. "What have you got there?"

"Nothing much," Hogsqueal said, pulling his hat down and trying to look innocent.

"Mew," his hat said.

"CAT!" Claw-Snotbelly gnashed his glass teeth. He rushed over, two other goblins right behind him. "Give it over. You gotta share."

"Catchers, keepers," Hogsqueal said. "You can't have it, Snotbelly. I got it first."

"What did you call me?" yelled Claw-Snotbelly. "My name is Claw! Claw!"

Those beetleknobbed goblins didn't look so dumb right then, Hogsqueal thought. They looked very alert and very angry. He realized that he better do something fast. He had two choices. He could give them the kitten or . . . or he could try to help it get away.

Which was dumb, because then no one

would have the cute, toothsome kitten.

But when he looked down into those big eyes, he didn't really want anyone to have it. He didn't really want to eat it. He just wanted to pet the silky fur and maybe see if he could get it to chase its own tail.

At that moment his hat fell, knocked off by tiny, batting paws. The goblins gasped. He could feel the cat's nails dig into his head.

Taking a deep breath, not quite sure what he was going to do until he started doing it, Hogsqueal turned and ran, one hand reaching up to grab the kitten. He tried not to mind when tiny claws sunk into his fingers.

He leaped onto a rusted bed frame, using the springs to launch himself at a refrigerator. He clambered up it, jumping down into a squishy pile of bags and moldering refuse on the other side. His feet sunk into the warm trash, making him stumble. The cat screeched.

The goblins followed. He could hear their ragged breath and feel their paws grasp at his coat.

He had to think of something to do, some better plan than putting one foot in front of the other. He just wasn't fast enough.

Passing a car, he tossed the kitten through the window, hoping the goblins wouldn't notice. Out of the corner of his eye, he saw the little ball of fur hit one of the leather seats. Its hair still stuck up along its back, but it immediately started licking itself with great dignity. He wished it had bothered to hide. Well, maybe if the goblins saw it, the choice of whether to grab for the kitten or grab for him would be so hard that they'd just stand around scratching their heads. A hobgoblin could hope.

He heard footsteps and grunting behind him. He dared a glance over his shoulder and it seemed they were all there, after him. But looking back slowed him down.

A claw closed on his leg, throwing him off balance. Falling on his face among bloated cans of pie mix and coffee grounds, he felt the weight of several goblins pile on his back. Two goblins grabbed his legs and arms. He couldn't move.

"Where's the cat?" they demanded.

Hogsqueal shrugged.

"Got it!" a goblin shouted, holding the furry creature aloft. The kitten mewed.

Figures, he thought. *All that for nothing.*

Hauling him on their shoulders, they carried him back to the goblin camp.

"Come on," Hogsqueal pleaded. "No hard feelings, cheeseheads!"

Ignoring his protests, they stuffed him in a birdcage, knotting it with vines before heaving it high into a tree. The hobgoblin looked down at the cages below him. Some of them were empty—others had miserable creatures scratching at the sides. He figured he must look as unhappy as they did.

The kitten's cage hung not far from where he was. The furry creature toddled around, yowling plaintively.

Serves you right, he thought, but its eyes still got to him. And it was awfully cute. Besides, all that noise would get on his nerves after a while, he was sure of it.

Reaching out, he could just touch the latch. He flicked it with a claw and the door sprung open. At first the little cat didn't seem to notice, but moments later it was clawing its way down the trunk of the tree.

He sighed. That was gratitude for you. All that trouble and the cat didn't look back even once.

Kicking his legs through the gaps, Hogsqueal swung his feet as he whistled a little tune. Okay, the accommodations weren't ideal, but something would come along. Something always did.

Hey, beetlebrains!
Do you want to learn more
about the noddy creatures
in these books?
Then turn the page. . . .

A Redcap Goblin

GOBLINS

FAMILY: *ADENTIDAE*

SPECIES: *Diabolus vulgaris*

PREFERRED HABITAT: Rocky outcroppings, caves, or even in ditches along the sides of the roads.

DESCRIPTION: Malicious and grotesque, a single *goblin* is a nuisance, but in large numbers they can be quite dangerous. Goblins travel in roving bands that scavenge for food and hunt smaller prey.

Their pranks run from distasteful to depraved. The rare goblin that is mischievous but good-natured is known as a hobgoblin.

Most goblin species are born without teeth. They must find substitutes, either the teeth of other animals, or sharp objects like glass, rocks, or metals other than iron. Masters of refuse, they are intelligent enough to make crude weapons.

Goblins have acute hearing and a highly refined sense of smell. Their large eyes can move independently of one another, and their smaller, simple eyes are capable of detecting body heat. Some goblins have bioluminescent organs on the tips of their tongues. These are used to attract sprites, their favorite food.

Brownies are small in size.

BROWNIES

FAMILY: *HOMUNCULIDAE*

SPECIES: *Custos domesticus*

PREFERRED HABITAT: On the land they protect (for example, an abandoned barn, an unused closet, or within the walls)

DESCRIPTION: These kindly and dependable creatures attach themselves to human households, where they help with chores and protect the well-being of people living on "their" land.

Fierce and loyal, *brownies* will defend a home and its surrounding estate against all foes. Despite their love of cleanliness, brownies are rather shabby in appearance, often going shoeless or wholly unclothed. Even so, they expect no payment other than scraps of food and a bowl of milk left out at night; in fact, further gifts are likely to induce adverse effects.

The careful observer may be able to spy one at work if he or she can sneak up quietly enough. Even if not actually seen, the brownie may disappear in the middle of completing a task, leaving proof in the form of half-finished mopping or partially washed dishes.